LESBIAN/ SAPPHIC ROMANCE 3

Age Gap Ice Queen CEO Romance

Maureen Lester

TABLE OF CONTENTS

Others in this series:

LESBIAN/SAPPHIC ROMANCE 2

LESBIAN/SAPPHIC ROMANCE 1

Chapter One

The Boss

Jackie Stevenson wakes to her alarm going off at its usual time of 5:40 am. Monday morning always comes too early and she struggles to get out of bed to start her day.

Jackie needs to make sure to get to work before her boss, Ms. Elsie Jacobs, to be ready for whatever she demands of her first thing.

46-year-old Ms. Elsie Jacobs is vice president of a large insurance company and Jackie is her executive assistant.

Jackie, being single and 24 years old, enjoys working closely with Elsie daily. Except for one thing...

Ms. Elsie Jacobs is the most peculiar combination of the frigid ice queen and shameless cunt tease Jackie has ever met in her life.

As Jackie begins her morning ritual, she thinks about her boss.

On the one hand, Elsie wears the shortest little skirts and the tallest high heels (the kind that drives Jackie crazy, with the thin straps around the ankles) to work each day, always leaving the top three buttons of her tight blouse open to reveal plenty of deep, creamy cleavage, and fastidiously keeps her make-up and long, dark hair as perfect as a Playboy Playmate ready to step in front of a photographer's camera.

Jackie arrives at work slightly before 8 am, with her coffee and espresso for Elsie, and waits for her arrival and what she had in store for her today.

Elsie is a very demanding boss and expects nothing but the best from Jackie. She is always very honest but can be extremely demeaning at times when she is displeased with her employees. Then she is curt to the point of condescension, her tone as warm as a February evening in northern Alaska.

Still, she has no qualms about leaning across Jackie's desk while the latter works to issue her orders, letting those ample tits hang down in front of Jackie's face, or bending over at the waist to retrieve something from a low shelf or drawer, so that the thin fabric of that skin tight, microscopic skirt rides as high up on her delicious rump as physically possible without exposing the panties whose lines are always so clearly defined beneath.

For Jackie, days at work are excruciating, her poor pussy as wet as water and her clit throbbing painfully and continuously against her panties from 8 am to closing time, without respite.

Jackie has taken to spending her coffee breaks and lunch hour in the bathroom, furiously fingering her beleaguered cunt to climax.

Unfortunately, no matter how often or thoroughly she relieves the agonizing tension in her throbbing clit, the moment she returns to her desk and tries to resume her work, she'd spy Ms. Jacobs climbing a step stool to retrieve something off a high shelf or absently fingering her nipple through her blouse as she combs through reports and Jackie's aching tits and clit would awaken with a vengeance.

Elsie arrives at her office at 8 am and greets Jackie with a sour, "Good morning," takes her espresso, walks into her office, and closes the door behind her. "Great," thinks Jackie, "she's in a wonderful mood."

After waiting about 15 minutes, Jackie

knocks on her office door. "Yes," she hears her say, as she opens the door and walks in. "Everything okay?" Jackie asks.

"Of course," Elsie replies coldly. "Well, I thought we should get started," Jackie continues. "You have a 9 am meeting, and we need to go over some final details beforehand."

Elsie looks up at Jackie with her beautiful dark eyes and says, very calmly, "Very well. But I'm sure I have all the details covered and am ready for my meeting." With that, she stands up and ushers Jackie out of her office and again closes the door to be alone.

The rest of the day doesn't go any better and Elsie takes whatever is bothering her out on Jackie any chance she can. Elsie finally leaves for home at 6 pm and Jackie can relax some before heading home herself.

She had heard Elsie talking to another

female exec about a blind date she had earlier in the week that didn't go very well. Something about her being a cold, insensitive bitch, or so that's what she was told by her date.

Jackie knew why Elsie was in a bad mood and wished she could do something to cheer her up, but she wasn't sure what that was or if she should even approach Elsie about it.

Chapter Two

Spying On The Boss

For whatever reason, Jackie decides to take a long way home that evening and drive through Elsie's neighborhood. Elsie lives in an upper-class neighborhood. It is after dark by the time Jackie pulls up outside her house.

None of the outside lights are on, and the house looks empty, except for one light coming out a window near the back of the house. Elsie's car is in the drive, so Jackie knows she is home, she just doesn't know if she should go up and knock, or what.

Quietly, exiting her car, Jackie decides to peek into her window to see what she is doing. She knows it is wrong, and a little voyeuristic as well. But Jackie thinks about all the days and weeks and months her boss had driven her insane with lust.

So, she looks around at the other houses and creeps around to the side of the house with the lighted window.

As Jackie crouches next to the window, she sees Elsie come out of her bathroom into her bedroom, clad only in a bathrobe.

Her long dark hair is loose and draped over her shoulders. Jackie thinks of how beautiful Elsie is as she gazes at her through the window. Her hair is damp and what skin she can see is still moist with water from the shower. She stands before the mirror in her room, brushes her hair, and releases the tie at her waist to allow the robe to fall open.

Jackie's jaw drops open. Her dry mouth begins to fill with saliva at the sight of her boss' long nipples jutting out of the robe, imagining them so close she can almost touch them.

Elsie stops brushing her hair, puts down the brush, and brings both of her hands to her body, opening the robe even more.

Elsie is still upset about her date and wonders to herself why she is still single at her age. "I'm still sexy, aren't I?" she asks nobody in particular as her hands wander over her large gorgeous tits, then her stomach and hips.

She shrugs off the robe and stands there naked before the mirror.

Jackie is amazed at the beauty before her. Elsie is taller than average, like Jackie, maybe 5'7" or so, and has long sensuous legs that end with a small patch of dark brown hair above her pussy.

As Jackie stands there fixed to the spot, her right hand wanders down between her legs and slowly strokes her slickness. Elsie's other hand is now cupping her massive breasts and gently pulling on her long nipples, making them stand even more at attention.

Soft moans escape her mouth and she closes her eyes as she starts to enjoy herself. "It's been too long," she thinks to herself.

She sits down on the edge of the bed, still facing the mirror, spreads her legs, leans back, and slowly slides a finger up and down her wet slit.

Pulling that finger to her mouth, she sucks it in, tasting herself. Elsie is oblivious to anything else going on around her, as her hand returns to between her legs and she moans as she slides two fingers inside her.

Her other hand tugs harder on her nipples as she pulls her expansive breasts to her mouth to lick each nipple in turn.

Laying back on the bed, now, both hands

between her thighs, Elsie continues sliding her fingers in and out of a now very wet pussy, while with her other hand, she begins to rub her clit from side to side. Biting her lip and moaning very loud, Elsie has a wonderful orgasm and continues to lie on her bed, her breath slowing down as her hands remain between her legs, gently rubbing her pussy.

As Jackie watches disbelieving but excited as these events unfold, her pussy lips are pulsing, her clitoris is swollen. She reaches into her panties and places a palm on her tortured sex. Her index and ring fingers caress her pussy lips, and the middle one dives between them, pushing against her erect button, before reaching down to the entrance of her hole with the tip.

Jackie is circling her fingers to the rhythm of her boss' movements. Her breasts are rising and falling in sync with Elsie's. She is sighing and moaning very quietly on the other side of the window, and forces herself to bite her lips.

Her hips begin to grind against her still fingers on their own, Her juices flowing down her legs.

Finally, Jackie takes deep breaths to calm herself down, then decides she better get out of there before one of Elsie's neighbors called the cops. Her cunt is throbbing in her panties, pussy dripping and she can't wait to get home and bring herself to climax.

Chapter Three

Surprising The Boss

Tuesday comes and goes at the office, as Elsie is out most of the day at meetings.

Even with her gone, Jackie has a hard time concentrating on work after what she witnessed last night. Jackie tries to keep herself busy, but images of her naked boss keep popping into her head. She can't wait till 5 pm to roll around, so she can head home and try relaxing. But, she wouldn't...

The whole of the following day, Jackie can't get the image of Elsie masturbating out of her head, but her boss was in such a foul mood it didn't matter.

Whatever happened yesterday at her meetings had put her in a very bad mood, which she takes out on Jackie all day.

Jackie just wants the day to be over quickly, so she can just get away from her for the night.

But after the day is done, Jackie thinks about what she can do to help her boss. Being the sly young woman that she is, she hatches a plan on the drive home.

Remembering the key to Elsie's house she had given Jackie when started work with her, Jackie strips down to nothing, grabbing her long trench coat, a strap-on dildo, and a mask as she rushes back to her car.

The mask is from last Halloween. As for the strapon dildo, it was a leftover from her last relationship.

Jackie reaches Elsie's home again, hoping for a follow-up masturbation session. She again quietly leaves her car in front of Elsie's house and sneaks up to the house.

Jackie stands at the front door, frozen, waiting. "But waiting for what?" She wonders. She has been to Elsie's house before for a holiday party, but can't remember the layout all that well.

She takes a deep breath, slides the key in as quietly as possible, slips the mask on, and opens the door.

The house is quiet and dark, just like the night before. Jackie hopes Elsie follows her previous night's routine.

As she creeps through the house, she hears music coming from the back corner and smiles as she sneaks up to the bedroom door, where she now hears the shower running as well.

Opening her bedroom door as quietly as possible, Jackie creeps into Elsie's room. The bathroom is to the left and she looks around for someplace to hide until Elsie comes out.

Jackie is making this up as she goes, realizing she isn't very good at it. She flips off the bedroom lights, hoping to catch her as Elsie goes to turn them on.

The shower stops and she can hear Elsie getting out. She jumps into a closet with a view of the bathroom, hoping Elsie can't see her. Keeping the door slightly ajar, Jackie waits and tries to calm herself down.

Elsie steps out of the bathroom and looks around suspiciously at her now dark bedroom. Not thinking anything of it, she starts to walk across the room to turn on the lights, when a hand grabs her and another covers her mouth before she has time to scream.

She is terrified. Struggling to get free she relaxes a bit when her captor speaks.

"Please don't, I don't want to hurt you." she hears him say in a very soothing way.

"Leave the lights off and don't scream. I promise it will be okay," she continues.

Elsie relaxes. There is something familiar about the voice, but she can't be certain; it is muffled, so it isn't clear. All she knows is that she is dripping wet from her shower and naked under her robe here in her bedroom with a stranger, and it excites her more than she cares to admit.

Adding to her excitement is the fact that she realizes from the pressure on her back that her strange visitor has breasts.

"Don't turn around and take off the robe." the voice demands.

Elsie starts to turn around as she drops the robe to the floor, revealing her still-wet naked body, when the woman behind her yells, "I said don't turn around!"

Elsie freezes. Excitement and fear both wash over her. "What did she want?" Elsie wonders.

Then the stranger is standing behind her and she feels her erect naked nipples press up against her back as her hands grab Elsie's nipples and twist.

Elsie wants to scream, but she also wants the stranger to keep going. Though she's never been with a woman before, it has been too long since she felt the touch of a man.

Jackie's hands roughly grab Elsie's breasts, the nipples hardening to the touch. Pushing Elsie towards the bed, she keeps her facing away from her.

Pulling a blindfold from her coat, Jackie wraps it around Elsie's eyes and ties it tight behind her head.

"No peeking." She whispers in her ear. A shiver runs up Elsie's spine as she shudders.

Jackie grabs one of Elsie's scarves and ties her hands behind her. Pushing her forward onto the bed, she pulls Elsie to a kneeling position and spreads her legs. Her boss' bulbous bottom sways gently back and forth in expectation.

Jackie reaches down with her hand and finds Elsie's pussy to be very, very wet.

She bends down next to her and whispers again in her ear, "You are enjoying this, aren't you, you naughty girl." Elsie nods her head up and down and replies, "Yes." in a weak whisper.

Jackie kneels behind her boss and inhales her scent. She had imagined how her pussy would look and is not disappointed as she spreads her cheeks and leaning down, she gently licks up the entire length of her pussy to her ass, even running her tongue along her asshole. A quiet moan escapes Elsie's mouth.

Standing again behind her, Jackie slips on the fake cock and positions it at the opening of Elsie's pussy. She slowly slides the cock inside Elsie.

Jackie grabs her hips, pulls out the cock till only the head remains, then slides it hard back into her. Over and over again, Jackie slides the cock almost out, only to slam the full length of the very thick, nine-inch staff back into her fist-tight twat. Elsie's moans become louder with each thrust of the cock.

The cold, aloof Ms. Jacobs is suddenly nowhere to be found, the ruthless cunt tease who'd driven Jackie to this desperate act, now moaning and urging her on like the rapacious whore she'd always dreamed she'd be.

"Oh God, fuck me, baby!" she shouts, eliciting even more merciless savagery from the one clutching her waist and filling her full of the very thick nine-inch cock.

"You're splitting me in half!" she cries as Jackie hammers ferociously into her velvet box. "Split me in half with that big fucking cock!"

All Jackie cares about is fucking this teasing, torturing bitch of a boss in her delicious little dick dock until she comes with a resounding crash. She is going to take it (and she is!), she is going to like it (and she does!), and she is going to be left wet and sore and sorry for all these months driving her batshit insane when she could have been getting this kind of deep, merciless dicking every goddamn morning!

As the world starts to go white and she feels the imminent ecstasy of release, Jackie does one last thing she's wanted to do ever since first getting hired by the alluring but alienating Ms. Jacobs – she pulls the cock out of her slippery cunt shaft and rams it right through the tiny opening of her anal sphincter.

"Oh oh OHHHHH!" cries Ms. Jacobs, her eyes clenching shut so tight that tears stream from them.

Jackie grins maniacally down at that incredible ass and sinks the entire enormous trunk into it, slamming hard against the dripping, gaping lips of her twat.

Ms. Jacobs suddenly convulses, every muscle in her body instantly petrifying, a long stream of spittle falling from the corner of her gaping mouth. The sounds that bellow forth from her throat are not words or even grunts, but guttural, primal exclamations, like the howling of someone who has completely lost control of their mental faculties.

She is cumming, harder and more violently than Jackie has ever seen anyone cum before, and she stands there pushing the massive cock as far up into Elsie's belly as it would go as she bucks and writhes and cums all over her.

Jackie sees a jet of liquid squirt from Elsie's cunt and splatters across her trench coat as Elsie contorts in ecstasy. Jackie's smile widens on her face.

Elsie comes again and again like that, squirting and flailing and roaring her unrestrained pleasure at the glorious agony of having her tiny little asshole ripped apart at the seams by a truly gigantic cock.

As close as she is to her own orgasm, Jackie now finds herself content to stand and watch as her brunette boss presses her ass back as hard as she can onto the impaling sword and blows her wad over and over again, each spraying, shrieking spasm more intense and feral than the last.

Finally, Elsie's curvaceous body goes limp and she slumps forward onto the bed.

The dildo-strapped intruder has had enough; the shaft of the shorter end of the double dong, tucked securely inside her own cunt, has rubbed and butted against the stem of her clit the whole time she is slamming into Elsie, and the constant friction serves to ignite an explosion of her own.

The Earth is crimson and swirling and Jackie is reeling from the mind-shattering orgasm.

The two women rest there for the next ten minutes or so in the same position. Finally, Elsie raises her tangled mass of hair and speaks.

"I don't even know your name, and I can't see your face."

A pause, and then a whispered response: "First I have to trust you. Then we'll see"

Jackie puts herself back together, then opens the bedroom door and is gone.

Elsie is left, naked, tied up, and blindfolded to figure out how to get loose on her own, her visitor's parting shot lingering in her mind.

Chapter Four

Naughty Boss Punished

The next day begins the same as the previous ones. Jackie arrives to work at her typical time; however, Elsie is already there. "Hope she's in a better mood today," wonders Jackie as she knocks on her door.

"Come on in, Jackie. Beautiful morning, isn't it?" Elsie asks with a beautiful smile.

"Good morning," replies Jackie with a returning smile as she hands her the espresso. "Yes, it is a beautiful morning."

"Well, I hate to ruin it so early, but you better cancel any plans you might have for tonight; it's going to be a long day," says Elsie.

"No problem. Didn't have anything special going on. What's up?" asks Jackie.

"Remember those reports you were working on earlier this week? Well, the deadline for those reports has been pushed up to tomorrow. I know, I know, you've been working hard, but we have to put the time in tonight to finish them," states Elsie as she looks up at Jackie with her beautiful brown eyes.

"Well, we better get working then," Jackie says as she smiles at Elsie.

The rest of the day is spent going over all of the details that Jackie has gathered earlier in the week to make sure that everything is accounted for. Everything is there, but something isn't coming together as it should be and both Jackie and Elsie are beginning to become frustrated. It is nearing 8 pm before either one of them realizes how late they have been working.

Jackie sits back, tired and frustrated. She

has worked too hard on this all week for something to go wrong, but it has. Elsie is fuming.

"How could you...I mean, you've had all week to pull this shit together, but..." she says glaring at Jackie. "We'll be here all night fixing this!" Elsie yells as she slouches down in the chair on the other side of the table.

Elsie just sits there across the table looking at Jackie with a pathetic look of disgust in her eyes.

That's it. Jackie can't take any more of this.

"Look, Elsie, I've worked my ass off this week for you, just like I do every day and I'm tired of you treating me like crap," yells Jackie back at her.

Elsie just continues to glare at Jackie from across the table, until a wicked thought comes to her.

"What are you going to do about it, Jackie?" she asks with an evil smirk. "Pull me over your lap and spank me?" she asks with raised eyebrows and a smile, knowing full well that her PA would not, even though they were completely alone in the office.

"Don't think I'm not tempted," replies Jackie with an evil grin of her own, not knowing where the hell this is leading to.

The room is silent as Elsie stands up, and walks around the table to the side where Jackie is sitting, to stand right next to her.

Looking down at her with those sexy, dark eyes Elsie asks, "What's stopping you?"

Jackie isn't sure what to do. Here was her boss, standing next to her daring her to pull her down over her lap and spank her. Jackie's mind is racing and replaying the scene from the previous night when she had fucked her boss' brains out.

Elsie interrupts her thoughts and asks, "Well, are you going to spank me or what? Haven't I been a naughty girl?"

Jackie doesn't have to be asked again. She reaches out, grabs Elsie around the waist, and pulls her down over her lap. Surprised, she lets out a squeal but smiles as she ends up with her ass facing up.

Jackie places her hand on her boss's ass and gently rubs her full ass cheeks through her skirt. Elsie turns back, looks at Jackie, and mouths the words, "Spank me."

Jackie raises her hand and it comes down hard on her ass. Even through her skirt it hurts, but Elsie likes it. Jackie looks at Elsie, and says, "It's about time someone treated you like this, but I think it would be better without the skirt, don't you?"

"What do you want me to do?" Elsie asks, innocently.

"Stand up and take off your skirt and blouse," replies Jackie, "and do it now!" she demands.

Elsie has never been treated like this before, until the other night, and she has never been more turned on than she is right now.

She can feel the dampness growing between her thighs as she begins to remove her blouse and skirt exposing her matching black lace bra, panties, and thigh-high stockings.

Standing almost naked before her young assistant, Elsie feels like the sexiest woman in the world.

"What now?" she asks, with her killer grin.

Jackie moves her chair back away from the table and motions for her to stand in front of her.

"Turn around and bend over the table," Jackie states.

Elsie looks at Jackie and wonders how far this will go. "Now!" Jackie demands.

Elsie turns around and slowly bends over the table in front of her assistant, spreading her legs slightly and grasping the other side of the table, her large gorgeous rump tilted upwards.

Jackie's left hand returns to her ass as she leans in and plants a soft wet kiss on her right butt cheek. Jackie raises her hand and with a much louder smack, it comes down hard causing Elsie to jump and scream.

Her butt cheek is red and Jackie rubs it to soothe the pain away. Both hands are now on her voluminous ass, as Jackie kisses the red spot she just caused.

She raises her left hand and with another loud smack, spanks Elsie again. The cheeks of her ass are both now red and the moistness between her legs is extreme. Elsie needs her to touch her there. She wants to feel Jackie's hands between her thighs. Elsie turns and looks at Jackie with pleading eyes.

Jackie has never seen anything or anyone as sexy as her boss before her. She continues to rub and lick her boss' ass.

Elsie reaches back and undoes her bra so she can tug on her long taut nipples as Jackie continues. Jackie pushes her chair back and kneels behind Elsie, her hands reaching up and slowly pulling her panties down over her full ass, till they were on the floor at her ankles.

Leaning in Jackie slowly licks from her clit to her ass with her tongue.

A low moan escapes Elsie's mouth as she

begs Jackie to continue. "More," is all she says.

Jackie raises her left hand again and Elsie braces for the spanking as Jackie's hand comes down again, harder this time. "God, that felt good," she thinks. Jackie licks the fresh red spot on her boss' great ass as both of her hands continue to wander over her backside.

Jackie's tongue returns to her boss' wet pussy, sliding in and out again and again. Elsie's moans become louder which encourages Jackie to continue. She slides two fingers deep inside her as she sits below her to suck on her clit.

Sliding her fingers in and out of Elsie, Jackie slides her tongue back and forth across her clit and Elsie comes for the first time that evening.

Chapter Five

The Next Level

Jackie stands up and sits on the table, moving slightly to the center where Elsie's chair is. She tells Elsie to sit in her chair.

Elsie obeys and sits naked before Jackie. Jackie bends down, grabs the arms of the chair, and pulls it towards her.

Elsie is now tight in between Jackie's legs and is now beginning to understand what Jackie wants. She is frozen in place as she watches Jackie begin to unbuckle her pants without being asked.

Then Jackie unbuttons his blouse as Elsie undoes her pants. Pulling them off along with her panties, her hard nub protruding slightly from underneath its hood awaiting Elsie's obliging mouth.

Jackie's ass rests on the edge of the table, as she is half sitting and half standing. Elsie wants to taste her young assistant, to return the favor, and hope to be as pleased with her cunt as she was with Jackie's tongue and fingers.

Aside from last night, Elsie has never been with a woman before although fantasies frequent her imagination of such.

Jackie lifts herself onto the table and places her feet on the arms of the chair. She parts her knees, which causes her pussy to open up, and Elsie can see she has moistened. Elsie looks closely a little anxious about what to do,

Jackie scoots forward a little more, pulling her feet to the front of the arms. Elsie can now see her asshole.

One of Jackie's hands finds its way to the back of Elsie's neck. Elsie feels some force as

Jackie starts pulling her head towards her cunt.

"Go ahead baby, taste me. Do it well. I take good care of you, don't I "

Elsie's head lowers until she's inches away from her. Jacy pulls her head harder until her mouth makes contact. Jackie lets out a sigh, "Ohhhhh yes that's it baby now lick it. "

Elsie shakes all over, blood fills her face, and she feels the heat. Her tongue leaves her mouth and tastes Jackie, Elsie can smell her, taste her, and these senses cause butterflies in her stomach.

Her tongue parts the lips of Jackie's cunt. Elsie slowly runs her tongue inside the folds of Jackie's lips moving it up and down her slit.

Elsie's clit now aches; she can feel a burning sensation, and her hips begin to move ever so slowly. Her hands move to Jackie's hips. Elsie moves closer inside Jackie's legs.

"Ohhhhh that's it, baby, oh yes that's it." Jackie moans as she speaks in a whisper, her voice is soothing and arousing.

Elsie begins to suck Jackie's cunt lips into her mouth, savoring them. They are wet, soft silky flesh. Jackie can not hold her hips still as they rotate about the table. Elsie finds her clit, and sucks it in her mouth flicking her tongue across it.

Jackie rotates Elsie's head as she sucks. Elsie becomes so hot from what she is doing. Jackie moves Elsie's head as though Elsie is involved in a deep French kiss.

"Oh suck it, baby, yes that's it suck it. " Jackie's breathing has grown heavier. Elsie feels Jackie's hand working the back of her head.

Elsie notices her own legs have parted and she is wet and swollen herself. She has moved one hand between her legs and starts massaging her clit as she sucks Jackie.

Jackie moans and whispers, "Don't stop. "

Elsie thinks Jackie must be near; Elsie moans and sucks her, "Mmmmmmmmm." Licking and sucking her clit now trying to drive an orgasm from her pussy.

Elsie moves her arm around the lower part of Jackie's back pulling her tight into her face. She begins to suck aggressively.

Jackie's hips begin to buck, she shoves her cunt into Elsie's face gasping, "Ohhhh Yesssss Oh God Yessssss." Bucking harder, "OH MY GOD YESSSSSSS OH GOD YESSSSS BABY YESSSSSS!"

Her bucking ceases her hips and her body quivers.

Elsie keeps licking, moving away from her clit and down to the opening of her cunt. She licks around the hole and then penetrates it.

Jackie lies back on the table now and starts rubbing her clit. Elsie notices that she has penetrated her own pussy with three fingers now running them in and out. Her hips move against her fingers as she fucks them.

Jackie whispers, "Move your tongue lower."

Elsie moves her tongue a little lower until she is at the lowest part of Jackie's cunt.

"Oh no baby, move your tongue lower. "

Elsie doesn't know exactly what Jackie wants so she starts kissing and licking the cheeks of her ass. They were so soft. The flesh of her ass cheeks excites her.

"That's it, baby, now lick my asshole." Jackie continues to finger her clit.

Elsie is so involved and so aroused. She moves her tongue to Jackie's asshole. Her heart picks up speed again, and Elsie is doing all kinds of things she has not done before. She is soaking wet between her legs. Her hips are viciously humping her fingers.

The minute her tongue touches Jackie's asshole, she lets out a moan, "Ohhhh yesssss baby oh yesssss that's what I like, baby...yessssssssss. "

Elsie starts flicking her tongue across it; Jackie's hips start rotating more now. Elsie keeps licking as her fingering becomes faster.

"God yes baby God Yesss do my ass baby. "

Her words have encouraged Elsie so that she puts her mouth over Jackie's asshole and starts French kissing it. This sends Jackie into a frenzy. She starts bucking her hips again, raising them off the desk now. Elsie takes both her arms and moves them under her thighs sliding them over her legs at the top. Elsie holds onto her tight.

Her mouth on her asshole tight now, French kissing it while she bucks, Elsie isn't going to let go. She holds on while Jackie furiously fingers her clit and bucks.

"YESSS... OH GOD YESSSSS... TONGUE MY ASS BABY... YESSS OHHH YESSSS FRENCH MY ASS BABY YESSSSS... OHHH GAWWWD!

She comes again, her quiver is violent as she grabs the hair on Elsie's head and squeezes. She relaxes back on the table for a few minutes and then raises herself. Elsie sits back up moving her fingers back to her cunt.

Jackie looks at Elsie smiling, "That was good."

Elsie looks into her eyes not saying

anything. Her hips are squirming in the chair. She has three fingers inside herself and the other hand massaging her clit.

"Don't stop, I want you to finger yourself looking at my cunt. I want to see you get off, I want you to get off looking at my cunt until you worship it."

She starts rubbing her clit again. She reaches down, grabs one of Elsie's hands, and moves it to her cunt.

"Slide your fingers in me while you get off. "

Jackie moves her pussy right close to Elsie's face, Elsie inserts two fingers inside her and starts to finger her own clit. She stares at Jackie's cunt; Jackie mesmerizes her; her fingers are soaking wet from her.

Elsie looks into her eyes; Jackie is staring at her. "That's it baby, cum for me. "

Elsie's hips squirm faster in the seat, her

fingers massaging her clit fast now. Her face inches from Jackie's cunt with Elsie's fingers inserted. Elsie looks up at her, she stares Elsie down, Elsie looks back at her cunt and can't take it anymore.

Her mouth goes to Jackie's clit, she sucks it in her mouth and starts bucking in her seat.

Elsie gasps and moans, "MMMMMM... NNNNNN... MMMMMMMM. "

She removes her mouth from Jackie. She comes violently in her chair, it is explosive. She soaks the chair.

Jackie pulls Elsie up and then lays her on her side on the table. While one of her legs is hanging off of the table, the other rests in the hands of Jackie, who holds it high, the ankle above her shoulder. She places her loins on Elsie's, letting their warm, wet pussy lips meet and kiss before pressing her button of joy against hers.

The smoothness of her skin against Jackie's pussy makes Elsie's pussy dripping wet with excitement as she feels Jackie start grinding herself into her. "Oh God Jackie..," she gasps, "...make me come."

They are moaning in unison. Their breathing speeds up. As their pace quickens, the splashing of lubricated cunt lips gets louder.

Elsie's erect nipples dance to the rhythm of Jackie pounding her. Then they reach for each other, their hands form a union, and their fingers clasp as puzzle pieces.

Then Jackie pushes her crotch against Elsie's and doesn't let her go. She keeps their clits snug with each other and presses their pussy lips together. Then she turns her head up to the ceiling and lets the orgasm shake her body, squirting some on Elsie's thigh. Elsie comes with her, howling in unison.

Chapter Nine

What's Next?

Elsie looks around at the mess they have created and looks at Jackie and they both start to laugh. "Guess we still have some work to do," she chuckles.

"Well, let's get cleaned up and get back to it, so we might get out of here at a decent time," replied Jackie.

They get dressed, clean up and go back to work and in no time, find the problem, have it fixed and decide to call it an evening. As they were getting ready to leave, Elsie stops Jackie, looks her in the eyes, and gives her a very long, deep wet kiss.

"Hope I was everything you imagined I would be," she says as they end the kiss.

"More," Jackie replies before they leave the

office together.

As Jackie drives home that night, she wonders if Elsie suspects anything from the previous night. Elsie drives home that night wondering if her assistant possibly is the masked woman that had taken her the previous night.

For now, they both smile as they make their separate ways home ...

...and they lived happily ever after.

THE END

\- **Maureen Lester**